For Alex and the snowstorm we drove through together.

Special thanks to Mi-Mi and Tien-Lih Chen and, of course, Max.

A BIG BED for LITTLE SNOW

GRACE LIN

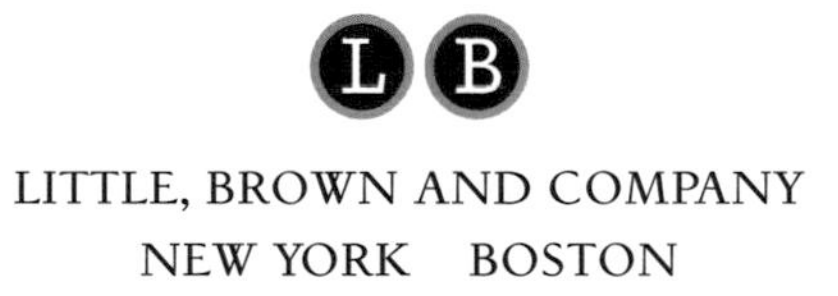

LITTLE, BROWN AND COMPANY
NEW YORK BOSTON

WHEN WINTER BEGAN, Little Snow's mommy made a big new bed just for him.

"Now you have warm feathers to sleep on," Mommy said. Then she looked at her little boy. "Remember, Little Snow, this bed is for sleeping, not jumping."

Little Snow grinned and nodded.

That night, tucked into his big bed,
Little Snow closed his eyes as Mommy
kissed him good night.

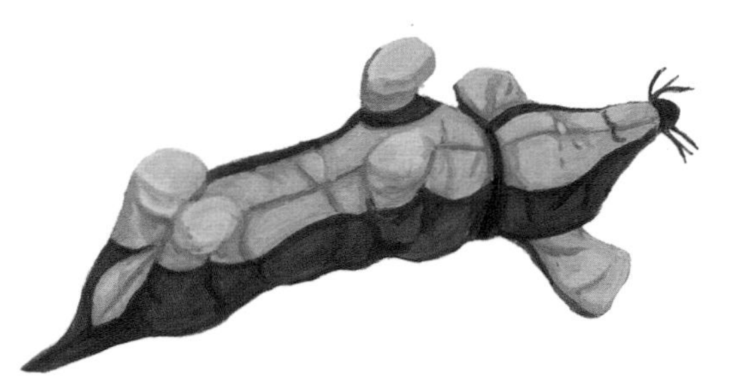

Thump,

thump,

thump.

Little Snow listened to Mommy's footsteps fade away.

Finally, it was quiet. Little Snow opened his eyes.

He rolled off his bed and looked at it.

His new bed was so puffy and big and bouncy!

Little Snow grinned and then

jumped,

jumped,

jumped!

Tiny feathers squeezed out of his bed and fluttered down.

Thump,

thump,

thump!

Uh-oh!
Was Mommy coming?

Little Snow flopped down on his bed.
"Little Snow!" Mommy said. "What are you doing?"
"Nothing!" Little Snow said, and he put his head back down on his big bed.

In the morning, when Little Snow woke up, he listened for his mommy's footsteps. It was quiet. Little Snow grinned and...

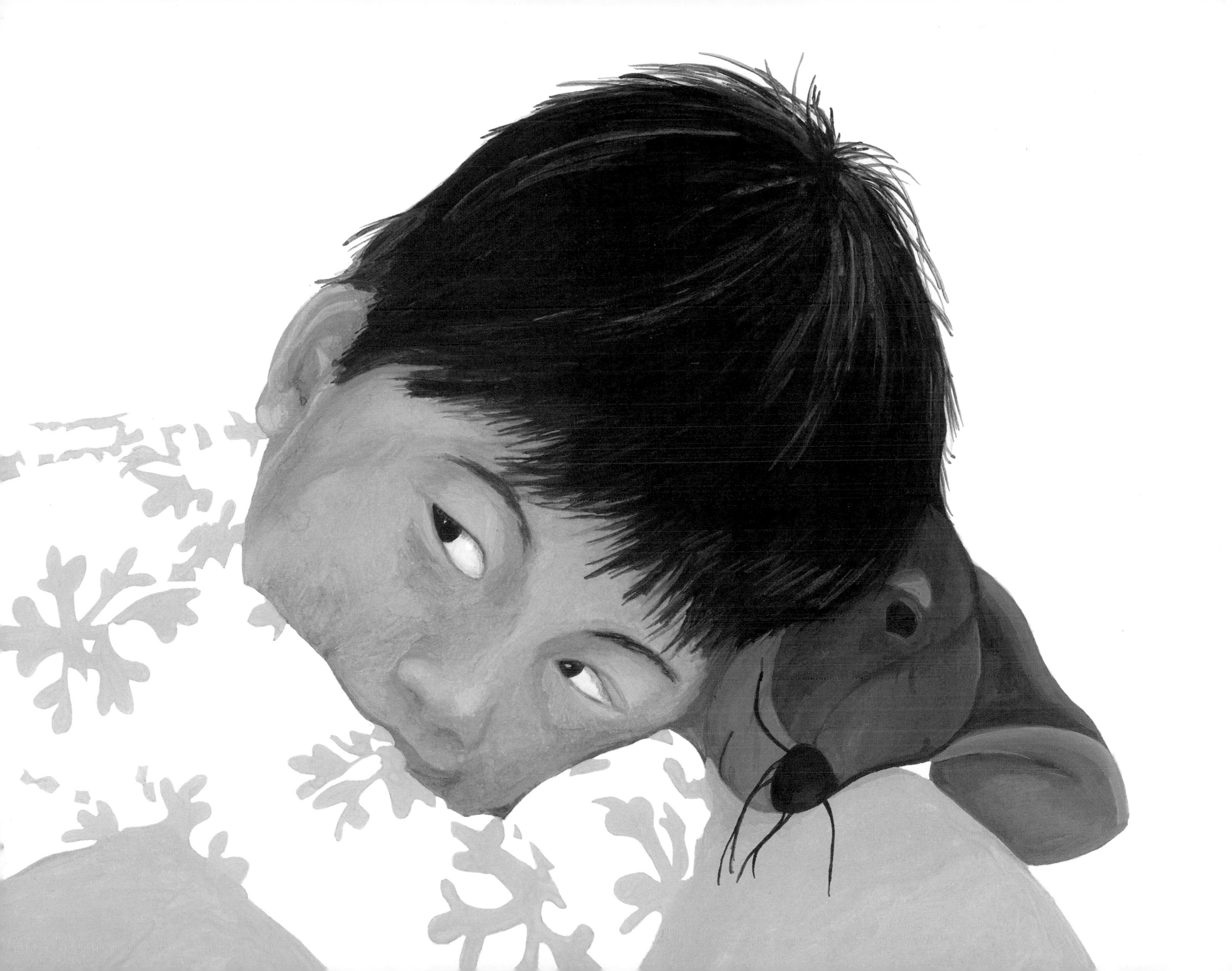

jumped

and **jumped!**

More tiny feathers fluttered down.

Thump,
thump,
thump!

Uh-oh! Was Mommy coming?

Little Snow flopped down on his bed.

All winter, whenever Little Snow was near his big bed,
he listened for Mommy's footsteps.

If it was quiet,
Little Snow grinned and then

jumped!

Sometimes, Little Snow jumped small, soft jumps.

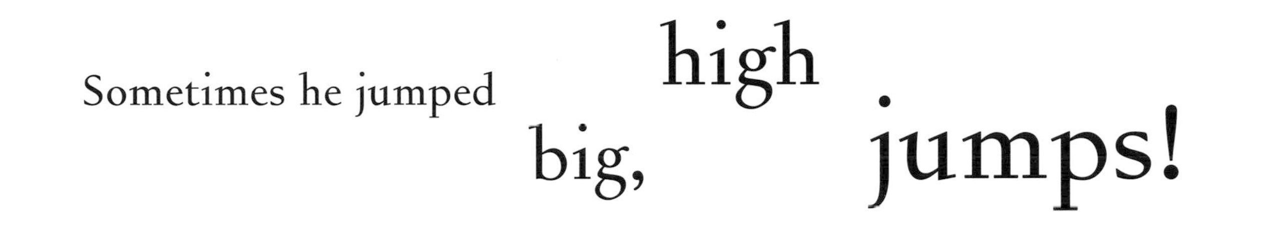
Sometimes he jumped big, high jumps!

Once, Little Snow jumped so high and landed so hard, he made a rip in his bed!

What a lot of feathers fell that day!

When winter was over, Mommy came to clean out the feathers from Little Snow's bed. But there were no feathers! Little Snow's bed was empty.

"Little Snow!" Mommy said. "Did you jump all the feathers out of your bed again?"

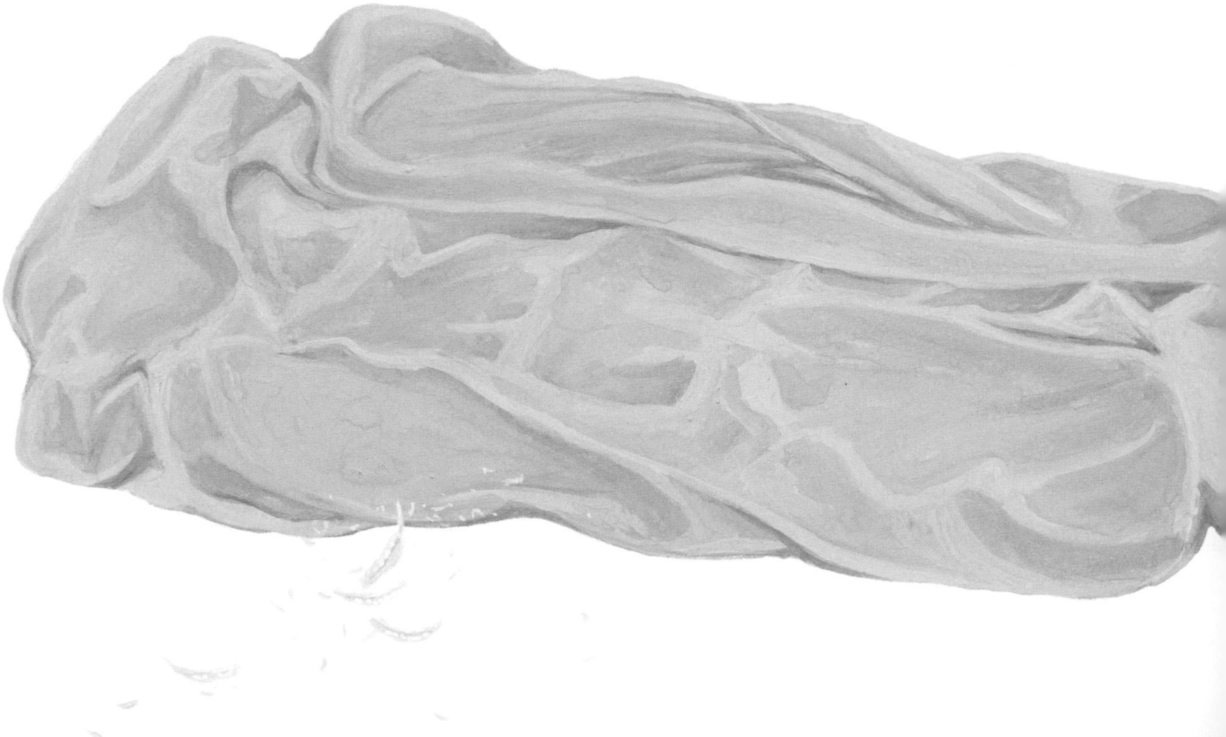

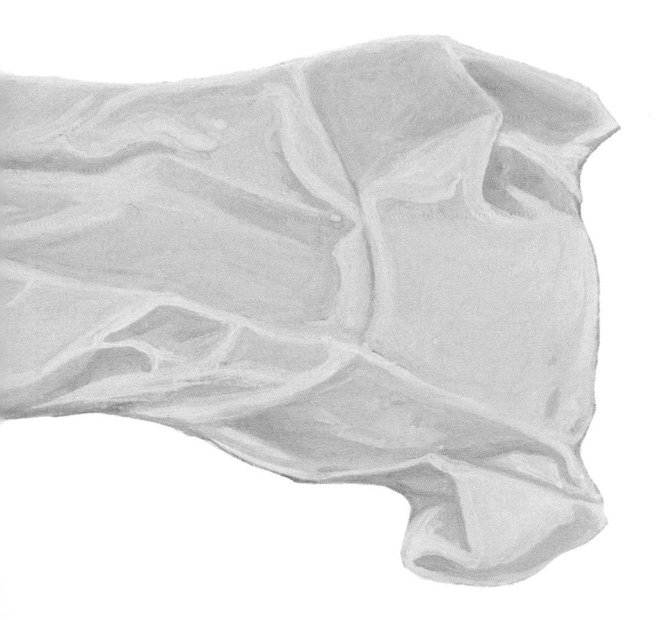

“Yes,” Little Snow said, but he grinned. “Aren’t you glad? Now all we have to do is fill it again next winter!”

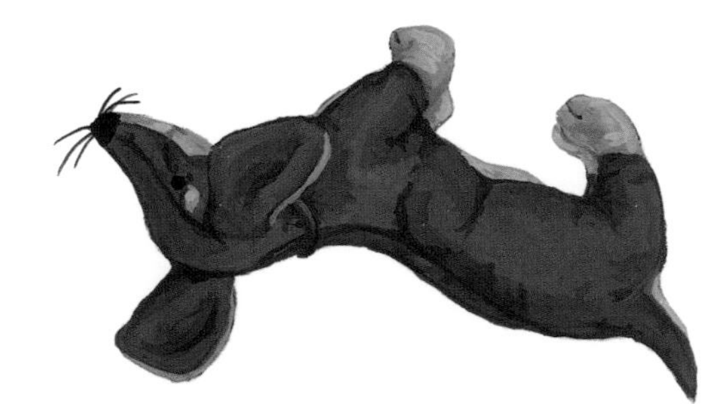

DISCARD